Ladies of the Throne

OBJECTS TALK BACK

About This Book Series

In collaboration with the Ethnologisches Museum and the Museum für Asiatische Kunst of the Staatliche Museen zu Berlin, the Stiftung Humboldt Forum im Berliner Schloss invited the writer Priya Basil to curate a series of events and books: *Objects Talk Back.*

Every year, Priya Basil asks two writers to engage with an object of their choice—either from the exhibited collection or from the museums' storage depot.

The project represents a new curatorial practice (complementing ongoing provenance research) characterised by transparency and dialogue regarding the collections in the Humboldt Forum, the complex history of its location and entanglements with contemporary global issues. The aim is to investigate the provenance history of the objects while simultaneously engaging in a direct dialogue with people biographically connected to the countries of origin, thereby fostering international multivocality and transforming museum practices.

Léonora Miano

Ladies of the Throne

HUMBOLDT FORUM

DIAPHANES

Ngwuo 'Mandu Yenu'
Throne chair made of wood, glass, textile, lime (cowrie shell)
Cameroon, Bamum, Cameroonian Grasslands
19th century
174 x 126 x 155 cm
Ethnologisches Museum – Staatliche Museen zu Berlin

Sultan Njoya of Bamum "gifted" this elaborate throne to Kaiser Wilhelm II during the German colonial period in Cameroon. However, in the context of such highly asymmetrical power dynamics, the term "gift" remains contentious. The throne is a significant cultural artefact and at the same time a symbol of colonial injustice.
Various collaborative research and museum projects are currently addressing the often violent histories of how cultural belongings from Cameroon were acquired. These initiatives foster dialogue and new forms of cooperation with partners and communities in Cameroon. A Cameroonian commission is currently working with eleven German museums to facilitate the restitution of cultural objects that were unlawfully removed during the German colonial era.

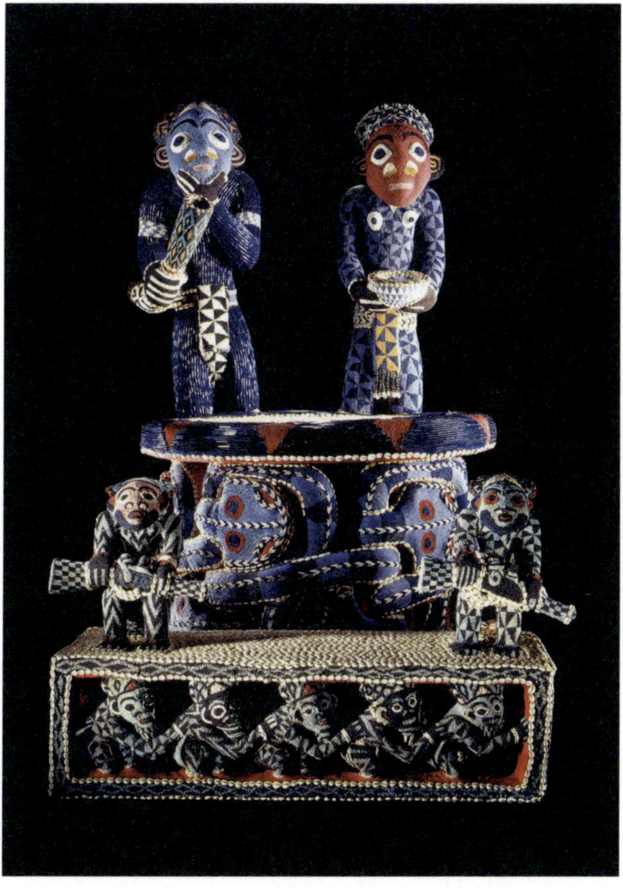

OBJECTS TALK BACK

Objects have voices, which we may not hear. Literature helps us to listen.

Objects Talk Back is a project that asks: what are the possibilities of literature to open up new stories, questions and relations when writers engage with museum archives?

While there are promising currents of change, ethnological museum collections remain tied to violent colonial histories and ongoing practices of domination. Information for most objects is still limited to date of creation or acquisition, place of origin, type of material, collector or donator. Even these details are not always accurate.

The archaeologist Dan Hicks proposes "necrography," a practice of digging into the past to trace the colonial story behind an object.[1] Such an approach may reveal much of value, but also leave one "straining against the limits of the archive," as literary scholar Saidiya Hartman writes.[2]

Colonial archives contain their own prejudices and distortions. Hartman suggests "critical fabulation"—melding history, theory and fiction—"to displace the received or authorized account." Inspired by these ideas, I coined the term "fabulography" for *Objects Talk Back*. In a piece for *British Art Studies*, I describe fabulography as an invitation to work creatively with-from-through gaps, facts and imagination to expand the narrative space around an object.[3] Fabulography involves digging deep, uncovering painful details, but also rising up, celebrating, honouring, re-connecting.

Since 2021, two writers are invited each year to explore collections of the Ethnological Museum and the Museum of Asian Art, both part of the Staatliche Museen zu Berlin. The writers encounter objects displayed in the Humboldt Forum, Berlin and also those stored in the museum depots. They select an object, and respond however they wish—through fiction, poetry, narrative non-fiction, multi-media texts. Later, they present the finished work at a live event in the Humboldt Forum.

Now, objects talk back in a book series as well, affirming Hartman's appeal "to consider stories as a form of compensation, perhaps the only kind we will ever receive."[4]

Priya Basil

1 Dan Hicks, "Necrography: Death-Writing in the Colonial Museum," *British Art Studies*, Issue 19, 2021: https://doi.org/10.17658/issn.2058-5462/issue-19/conversation | **2** Saidiya Hartman, "Venus in Two Acts," *Small Axe* (Indiana University) 12, no. 2 (2008): https://muse.jhu.edu/search?action=browse&limit=publisher_id:3 (accessed March 9, 2024). | **3** Priya Basil, "Writing to Life," *British Art Studies*, Issue 19, 2021: https://www.britishartstudies.ac.uk/issues/issue-index/issue-19/death-writing-in-the-colonial-museums (accessed March 9, 2024). | **4** Saidiya Hartman, "Venus in Two Acts."

Priya Basil

Introduction

In all Léonora Miano's writing, the past speaks—through people, objects, ritual, ceremony, language, spirit, other life forms. Her oeuvre is hailed as a territory freed from the Western gaze, yet its landscapes are filled with shadows. "The shadow is also the shape our silences take," she writes in *Season of the Shadow*. Towards the end of that novel, one character shares with others some knowledge that has been relayed to her: "The woman says that you cannot dispossess people of what they have received, learnt, experienced. They themselves could not do so, even if they wanted to. [...] The ancestors are here and they are not a confinement. They conceived a world. This is their most precious legacy: the obligation to invent in order to survive."[1]

The *Objects Talk Back* team at Humboldt Forum were first in touch with Léonora Miano in April 2021, when the Covid pandemic was still at its peak. It was not clear when travel restrictions would ease and if a research trip to Berlin would be possible. So, Léonora Miano initially received a list of objects connected to Cameroon held by the ethnological museum in Berlin. *Objects Talk Back* never proceeds from the assumption that writers select objects from territories related to their personal biography or background. The premise is, rather, a recognition that writers come with expertise and knowledge of certain places, times, cultures, languages; knowledge gained through their work, as well as through lived experience. This offers initial orientation for encounters with the museum collections, and the writers may continue in any direction. Léonora Miano requested a more expansive list of African objects and asked, "Are they wanted back home?" She elaborated: "I believe it would be better to write about artefacts that are actually wanted back, though it does not have to be mentioned in the text. We do not want to give the impression that each and every African object was wrongly acquired or that cultures from the Global South have no place in Western museums."

Born in Douala, Cameroon, in 1973, Léonora Miano is one of the most important voices in francophone literature. A novelist, playwright and essayist, she is the author of nearly twenty books which are a testament to her beautiful language, supreme storytelling and expertise on ancient African cultures. She has received numerous awards, including the prix Femina and the Grand prix du roman métis in 2013 for her novel *Season of the Shadow*. The English translation was published to great acclaim in 2018. Her work has been translated into many languages.

Léonora Miano conceptualized and curates the *Quilombola!* book series. It is, in her words, "a space from which resonate insubordinate, inventive, provocative and unexpected voices." The series is published by Seagull Books. Miano is also the founder and director of The Quilombo Publishing based in Lomé, Togo, where she now lives. "*Quilombola* is a Brazilian word for the inhabitant of a maroon or 'runaway-slave' community," Miano explains. "The choice of this appellation is a tribute to those who, throughout human history, have stood up against oppression. However, there is more in this reference: it speaks both about freedom regained and about all the creative gestures that stemmed from that conquest. For those who had broken their chains, the *quilombo* was a place of reappropriation and reinvention of oneself."[2]

As it turned out, Miano was able to visit Berlin in August 2021. The Mandu Yenu throne had just been brought into the exhibition room at the Humboldt Forum and was being unpacked for a new permanent exhibition. The throne step was still partly in a crate. The throne seat, with its two attendant figures, was on a wooden trolley, waiting to be wheeled to the right spot amidst other objects that were under sheets or part-installed. Even so, the throne had tremendous presence. Its powerful allure affirmed the decision toward which Miano had already been inclining: this would be the object.

A throne is a seat of power. The nature of power is one of the central themes of Miano's writing. Whether she is examining colonialism, racism, feminism—it's always the nature of power relations, the destructive or creative possibilities of power that she turns over and over. She extends this approach in "Ladies of the Throne," showing how, as she says in an essay from the book *Sisterhood*, "on our continent the women were everything a human being could strive to be. They were light or shadow, sometimes both. Without them there would simply be no history."[3]

Léonora Miano's work makes imagination a tool for

inventing, stories a form of surviving. Her writing preserves, revives, recreates other ways of being, seeing and doing; it enacts the Quilombola spirit. From this spirit a new narrative around the Mandu Yenu throne emerges.

"Our continent has of course its instruments of protection. [...] They are now imprisoned in Northern Museums," Léonora Miano writes in her novel *Twilight of Torment: Melancholy.*

"The Northerners don't know how to use them. Sequestering them as they have has enabled them to take advantage of us. For centuries. They've no desire to return them. Some argue it would be useless. Not because we lack adequate structures to preserve them. That's a mere material question. Easy to resolve. There's no point, they maintain, because we've forgotten what these objects used to say. My conviction is that they would speak to us again if they were given back to us. They'd find us once more."[4]

1 Léonora Miano, *Season of the Shadow*, trans. Gila Walker (Kolkata: Seagull Books, 2018), pp. 30 and 235. | 2 Léonora Miano, *Quilombola!*, https://www.seagullbooks.org/books-by-series/quilombola/ (accessed October 4, 2024). | 3 Léonora Miano, *Sisterhood. Für einen anderen Dialog zwischen den Frauen der Welt* (Berlin: Aufbau Verlag, 2022), p. 91. Translation by Priya Basil. The original title is *L'autre langue des femmes* (Paris: Grasset, 2021).| 4 Léonora Miano, *Twilight of Torment: Melancholy*, trans. Gila Walker (Kolkata: Seagull Books, 2022), p. 90.

Léonora Miano

Ladies of the Throne

From Feminized King to Women of Influence

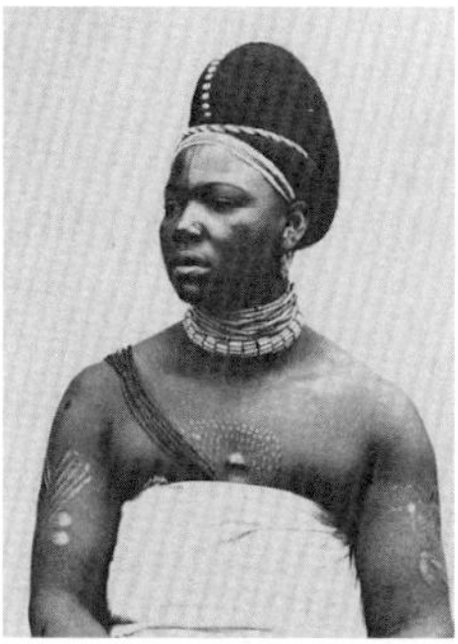

Unknown Woman from Foumban.
Photographer Unknown.

Most of the time, it is the power of men that we remember. It is a matter of their prestige that streams onto the people they govern: the monarch's bearing and the pomp of his court are purported to spill over onto those over whom his authority is exercised, including within highly hierarchical societies, and even slave societies.[1] The same is the case for the Kingdom of Bamum, a small territory of around eight thousand square meters. In Cameroon where it is situated, the Kingdom of Bamum is associated with a masculine figure. King Njoya may not have been the most flamboyant monarch of his people, but he was the one who interacted with the colonialists, the one who appeared in their archives and whose reign was partly documented. Moreover, Njoya devised a system of writing and set out to record the history and customs of his kingdom. When Cameroonians who are not from this part of the country refer to him, that is what comes foremost to mind. By one of those peculiar ironies to which history holds the key, this monarch, who was attached to the memory of his people, was the one who relinquished his father's Mandu Yenu[2] to please his German allies. He was the last Bamum king to govern a sovereign state—well-structured, powerful and prosperous—and the one whose thirty-eight-year reign, marked by the colonial presence, witnessed the imposition of a new administration that stripped him of his power.

Having chosen to collaborate with German colonizers in order to preserve his lands and his power, King Njoya was exiled by the French when they took control of Cameroon. He died under house arrest, far from his kingdom, separated from his people. To the French, he was a slave-holding despot, a megalomaniac who persecuted Christians, and the organisation of the Kingdom of Bamum was incompatible with their colonial project. They therefore applied themselves to dismantling it. These two sides of the same coin serve the posterity of the man. By its brutality and its humiliating character, the treatment inflicted by the French colonizers on the Bamum monarch make of him a victim, not so much of the rivalries between European powers as of the colonial order as a whole. The younger generations, who know little about these matters that are not well covered in the school curriculum, need to be given information that will enable them to grasp the complexity of historical facts.

Ibrahim Njoya's collaboration with Germany, which allowed him to maintain his authority over his subjects, had grave repercussions on the activities of the resistance and resulted in the execution by the Germans of Rudolf Duala Manga Bell, Adolf Ngosso Din, Madla ma Dimale, and Marin Paul Samba on August 8, 1914. Njoya had notably told the Germans about their plans for an uprising. Invited to join the fight against the Germans, the Bamum monarch did not confine himself to refusing; he went so far as to denounce the revolt. Njoya lived through two different colonial systems. The German model, which focused on economic exploitation, did not seek to change the Bamum social structures and left them intact. Under this regime, which did not encroach upon his legitimacy, his territory,[3] or his traditional prerogatives, *mfom*[4] Njoya was a monarch open to all manner of foreign practices, be it in the area of new techniques, religion[5] or even botany, since he experimented with new seeds.

Like other sub-Saharan monarchs throughout the long history of the encounter between Africa and

Europe, Njoya was curious about European advances and thought he could gain a little of the power of these foreigners through association with them. In his case, this strategy was manifested even before the European presence in his kingdom. Threatened at the time of his enthronement, Njoya turned to the Fulani for help in holding on to the Mandu Yenu. After his victory, he sought to acquire the power that permitted his allies to triumph:

> In fact, between 1898 and 1908, a conversion to Islam had taken place. This happened after the intervention of the Fulani of Banyo solicited by the young Njoya who had just ascended to the throne and found himself in the throes of a civil war. The "victory of the horse" prompted the king to invite the Islamized Fulani to send marabouts. It also prompted him to elaborate a script, which was done some time later.[6]

In this way a variety of Muslim practices made their appearance in Bamum society, without the traditions inherited from the ancestors being abandoned. For the man who became Sultan Njoya, this was by no means an identity or cultural question, which was something that never came up. All that interested him was power, that is, whatever enabled him to remain in control of his kingdom in a tumultuous world. When foreign practices could endanger the ancestral culture, the power inherited from his predecessors, they were not adopted. For example, Christian missionaries never managed to convert the Bamum king, since that would have meant getting rid of hundreds of wives,[7] and even abdication.

Obviously, between the Bamum monarch and the Germans there could be no egalitarian collaboration, but rather a rational understanding between parties who were well aware of the forces at work. When the foreigners arrived on his lands in 1902, Njoya took a stand against the people in his entourage who wanted to go and fight them. He asserted that in his dream he had seen the coming of the Germans and the crushing defeat that his people would suffer if they went to war. The fact that none of the neighboring peoples had succeeded in defeating the Germans was grist to his mill. The policy he favored instead involved being welcoming and conciliatory toward the new masters of the kingdom. Aboubakar Njiasse Njoya, grandchild of the sultan, writes that his illustrious ancestor compared himself, in his dealings with the Germans, to a woman faced with men, a situation that left him no choice but to obey them.[8] If he ended up giving them one of the Mandu Yenu, after having long refused to comply with their request, it was because he felt constrained to do so.

In a context of impotence vis-à-vis an interlocutor that one knows cannot be defeated, gifts are tributes that do not say their name, especially when the object given is of such symbolic, quasi-sacred value. Collaborating with the Germans, *mfom* Njoya may have seen no problem in denouncing the anti-colonialist resistance of the kings from other regions of Cameroon. After all, Cameroon was a pure European creation, as are many of today's sub-Saharan countries, and had nothing much to do with his roots and his filiation. Njoya's country was first and foremost that of his ancestors, a territory expanded and made prosperous by its eleventh king, Mbuombuo, who gave Bamum society its physiognomy. On the other hand, the idea that he gladly gave away a Mandu Yenu is frankly inconceivable.

Of what interest is the throne of the Bamum kings today, beyond its aesthetic qualities and its symbolic value? It is no longer the object itself but the history of the men who stood on either side of it that should be read between the lines of beads and cowrie shells. On one side were those whose persistent greed did not relent before what their interlocutors would consider precious, untouchable and non-transferable. On the other, those who refused to let go of a sacred piece, convinced that doing so would bring misfortunes upon them, which in fact were not long in coming. Practically speaking, from the time of their arrival in Bamum country, the Germans, in their eagerness to fill their museums and homes with objects testifying to their domination over African lands, coveted the throne of the Bamum.[9] The piece is sumptuous, imposing and rare. It is, moreover, of particular significance. The importance of art for the Bamum people, the majesty of the objects produced in its workshops, are well known to collectors of this period. Anyone interested in sub-Saharan artefacts can immediately recognize the very characteristic style of the Bamum. Under *mfom* Njoya, the artisans of the kingdom worked to satisfy the European demand, and objects were designed for the foreign market.

To signal the alliance and consolidate good relations with those he'd seen in his dream overpowering his people, Njoya offered many objects, some imposing. The Mandu Yenu of King Nsangu, his father, is the only piece he refused to part with, even when he was offered a thousand marks to sell it, plus the Kaiser's throne in exchange.[10] All of the stratagems devised to secure the one object that the Bamum didn't want to give up at any cost shifted to the symbolic ground a war that was not fought using weapons. For the Bamum, considering the nature of the object, giving a throne, selling it or exchanging it boiled down to the same thing. It meant abandoning an essential part of themselves, surrendering a piece of their soul, dooming themselves to never be the equal of those who obtained such a capitulation from them. There can be no friendship between colonizer and colonized. Cordial exchanges do not erase the reality of the type of relationship that colonial domination forges. Quite the opposite: no attempt to smooth over the edges can make them less cutting. There is something that makes this situation seem even worse than forthright violence inflicted upon the subjugated. At least then you know what you're up against.

The question of whether the Mandu Yenu on view at the Humboldt Forum in Berlin is a replica or an original is meaningless. For those who made it, the throne represents something that is not duplicated. Once it is decorated with beads, it is the Mandu Yenu, the throne of Bamum rulers since Mbuombuo, the eleventh *mfom.* Two versions of it are always made. It takes several months, sometimes up to nine, to do so. A special wood is used, to which the Bamum attribute protective powers. The craftsmen carving the throne are not making a piece of furniture, but an object symbolizing both the power of the *mfom* and the bond that unites him with his people.[11] The human figures represented on the seat and the footstool serve, support and accompany the monarch. The Mandu Yenu is consecrated in the course of a ritual ceremony convoking the spirit of deceased kings, before being blessed. Who deliberately parts with a consecrated object? All the more in that the Bamum sovereign is invested during his enthronement with the spirit of the one who preceded him. In this way, he becomes part of a chain of succession in which he is the living figure of all those who ruled before him.

> From that moment, and by virtue of the tradition that the successor is not only an heir to the rights of his predecessor but that he succeeds the person of his predecessor and identifies with him, the king who has just been put on the throne identifies with the whole line of Bamum kings and could be addressed by the name of the kingdom's founder, Nchare: in the eyes of the Bamum he was Nchare.[12]

After having frequented this Bamum king for several years, we can assume that the Germans were not ignorant of the more important aspects of his culture. Be that as it may, *mfom* Njoya's continued refusal should have prompted them to relent. They had before them a man who, to prove his loyalty, had not refrained from denouncing the anti-colonialist resistance, covering his hands in so doing with the blood of Cameroonian martyrs. The Germans left Bamum culture intact but they did not respect it. What the Bamum treasured was nothing but merchandise to the colonizers.

Did *mfom* Njoya, who felt like a woman in his relationship with the Germans, remain a king to his people in the full sense of the term? In the kingdom of Bamum, women do not normally sit on the throne and the public face of the sovereign is expected to be powerful and glorious. It is in private life that a gentleness qualified as feminine is considered welcome from him.[13] Given the misadventure of the Mandu Yenu that ended up being handed over to the Germans and exhibited from then on in their museums—when they were only very rarely presented to the Bamum themselves and then only on very specific occasions—it seems that colonization brought the private figure of the king into the public arena. The colonized Njoya, who defended in vain the sacred throne of his fathers only to part with it in 1908, became a monarch whose authority had been compromised. Not because he lost his subjects' respect, but because he himself considered that this was the case and felt that he was a woman, and hence forbidden from governing according to the view of the Bamum. The king may well be regarded as father and mother of his people—with the second aspect being bound up with the nurturing function of power—but this symbolic androgyny must be maintained and each of the polarities expressed in the appropriate environment.

Didn't handing over the Mandu Yenu to foreigners amount to depriving himself of the strength of the male ancestors whose spirit he harbored and whom he represented? Didn't he consent in so doing to making their legacy obsolete, invalidating it in a single gesture? For this king who was so concerned with the posterity of his fathers that he himself put their history into writing, such a deed was no doubt much more serious than the denunciation by which he became complicit in the execution of anti-colonialist fighters. In his own eyes, Njoya felt he'd betrayed his people and, after that, there could be no way that history would remain favorable to him. And indeed it wasn't. It should be noted that no premonitory dream warned the king of the German defeat in the Great War, of the arrival of the English who stayed only a year in Bamum territory, still less of the coming of the French who blew his power to pieces. The great Bamum of the past had apparently ceased to speak to their descendant to reveal dangers on the horizon and the measures to take. The feminization of the king took place in two stages. The first was the submission to foreigners and his decision not to join forces with others as he had done to defeat his opponents during the civil war at the start of his reign. The second, which followed from the first, consisted in parting with the Mandu Yenu of his father, King Nsangu. From a certain standpoint, Njoya was a woman in power, which the tradition of his people did not authorize save in certain very specific circumstances.

The feminization that Njoya's own grandson speaks of, attributing the words to his ancestor, leads us to question the real place of women in the Bamum political arena. When it comes to the throne, let us reiterate that it is in principle inaccessible to women. If ever a woman took a seat intended for the monarch, it was on the sly, and surely a woman with a good upbringing would never consider doing so. Yet, although women did not govern in principle, they were not absent from the history of the Mandu Yenu or of Bamum power. In reality, if the object stills holds a real interest in our time, it is also because it brings us to these women and compels us to draw them out of silence. The name of the throne itself invites us to do so, since Mandu and Yenu were two royal wives of the king Ngulure. Yenu, the elder, was one of the oldest wives, perhaps among the first. The two women had great affection for one another and their age difference did not stand in the way of their friendship. When the king told Mandu that he wanted to designate one of their sons as successor, Mandu refused and suggested that he choose Kuoto, Yenu's son.

Ngulure heeded his young wife's advice and, when he died, Kuoto became the tenth king of the Bamum. Following tradition, the new monarch, who thenceforth inhabited the identity of his predecessor, inherited the latter's young wives. Mandu was among them. She knew that it would be so. They had three children together. To thank her for having supported his mother and hence himself, the king chose Mbuombuo, Mandu's second son, to succeed him. Mbuombuo, the eleventh Bamum king, was flamboyant, inventive and a conqueror. He was the one to have the first Mandu Yenu made. Naming the throne after his mother and grandmother was a tribute to the friendship without which he would not have been king. We do not know if his intention was also to underline the role of women in Bamum royalty, but the result is undeniable. Bamum kings are always born to royal wives. Such women must have no captive ancestry, since the servile condition rules out the exercise of power.[14] Kings can also be the sons of "princesses of blood" and, as the above story indicates, women's voices were heeded when it came to their designation. Thus, deprived in principle of the physical embodiment of power, they nonetheless contributed to making kings. When a king was enthroned, he chose among his brothers two viceroys, but also a woman who was called *momamfom*.

The third personage of the kingdom after the king, the *momamfom* symbolizes its femininity. This princess may not sit on the throne, but she is regarded as having a share in the royal power and she is one of the principal advisers to the king. As elsewhere in sub-Saharan Africa, without necessarily allowing women to rule, Bamum society does not imagine that it can function well without their voices being heard. In the court of the Bamum king, in addition to the domestic functions of women common throughout the world yesterday and today, they are responsible for the protection of sanctuaries and—

an uncommon fact that is important to note—there is a female guard.[15] The mission of the guard unit is defense and those who are part of it are trained for combat. In contradistinction to what can be observed on other continents, in Europe for instance, femininity is not seen here as being limited to grace and gentleness. Authority, severity, the search for material goods and warlike qualities, for example, are accepted from women who manifest these characteristics. Two wives and mothers of kings evidenced this in a quite spectacular way.

The first, whose name was Ngungure but who called herself Chetfon, was the daughter of King Mbuombuo, the mother of King Nsangu, and the grandmother of Njoya. She stands out in Bamum history for having sat on the Mandu Yenu, albeit for not more than half an hour. Being the only one in a position to transmit the power to her son, she was seated on the throne for the time it took to effect this transition. Chetfon, the name that she chose to carry, means "the one who surpasses the king." In taking this name, she wanted to signal the anteriority of her royalty over that of the *mfom*. She was a wealthy woman, who owned seventeen plantations, had her court and her people—a community of three thousand souls.[16] Chetfon was known for her generosity, humor and friendliness, but also for her involvement in affairs of the state and her influence on her people: "When she spoke of war to the Pamɔm, they listened to her with more respect than to the king. She spoke of it with great force. She spoke of it in the way a man does."[17]

Chetfon was thus the de facto queen. She did not bear the title for longer than the thirty minutes she was seated on the Mandu Yenu, but King Nsangu's mother had power. To "speak of war" does not mean, of course, to tell the story of past wars, but rather to say whether it was opportune in the present to go to war, against whom and in what way. In all periods and in all places, this is royal business par excellence. Speculations in this regard may be pointless, but one cannot help wondering how this woman would have reacted to the foreigners wanting to take the throne of the Bamum kings back to Germany with them.

The difference between a feminized king and a powerful woman is self-evident. Whereas the former is demeaned, the latter is in full possession of a power that derives from both her social status and her own temperament. Judging from her marital and love life, Chetfon was not a conventional woman. Indeed, she divorced five times, which has the merit of teaching us that the thing was accepted. After the last divorce, she didn't remarry but had several amorous relationships.

Bamum princesses were reputed to enjoy great sexual freedom. But Chetfon was a royal wife, not a princess. As such, she was forbidden from having intimate relations with anyone except the *mfom*. Death was the penalty for those who transgressed this law, which she always vehemently denounced. Chetfon saw several of her lovers die as a result. She sought a kind of companionship that wasn't granted to her, and each of these losses made her sink into depression. After one of these terrible bereavements, there was even fear she'd commit suicide, which indicated the intensity of her search for a love relationship and the sincerity of her feelings for these men. And they must have shared her passion, since they were not ignorant of the law and took the risk nonetheless to be put to death. Being an important person in the kingdom, Chetfon's amorous passions could hardly be dissimulated.

It was not without reason that the Bamum imposed such heavy prohibitions on the sexuality of royal wives, whereas the princesses and even the mothers of the *mfom*'s wives lived more freely. Because they had access to the king's private life, royal wives could not be touched, they could not give their belongings to others, one could not drink from their cups, etc. There was a fear of poisoning, of the transmission of diseases that could have affected the king without the exact provenance being known. This strict law applied even to those that the *mfom* had not yet known, since access to his bed was rare for a great number of them. It was also a matter of not reducing the king to the rank of commoners, and so those who had belonged to him could not belong to others. In the case of Chetfon, who had divorced several times, some flexibility could have been expected, but she was a woman. And the fact is that, from a conservative perspective on heterosexual relations that hasn't disappeared, a woman gives herself to a man who possesses her and not the other way around. In giving herself to men, the royal wife is offering the king's property, even the king's body. She is a Mandu Yenu of a particular kind: that of the private arena, of nudity, of the purity of royal blood. This is even more the case if she has not gone through menopause and can still bear children. The sexual act is also believed to have a mystical dimension, which exposes the woman to mortal dangers. This is what the king intimated when Chetfon protested once again after one of her lovers was executed.[18]

If Bamum law seemed excessively harsh to Chetfon insofar as her love life was concerned, she was not squeamish when it came to resolving problems. Her son Nsangu lost his life on the battlefield. "The one who surpasses the law" did her duty by pointing to who was to succeed her, specifying that she was at the origin of the choice. Then, to defend her son's honor from accusations that he took women who were not his to take, Chetfon killed them with her own hands. There were twelve of them. The reasons that she put an end to her life thereafter remain obscure. It has been observed that two of the deceased king's sisters hung themselves when they heard news of his death in the war. Suicides such as these are rare in sub-Saharan societies where life is revered above all else, regardless of the conditions, and they draw attention to the singularities of the Bamum world. Filled with intrigues, like all circles of power, the royal court of the Bamum has its mysteries. In his *Histoire et coutumes des Bamum*, Njoya is not very precise about a good many matters. A king is not a historian. Be that as it may, in the section titled "the book of the mothers of kings," the extensive attention given to Chetfon is most remarkable. Wife and mother of kings, her personal qualities were what made her loved and respected, thereby consecrating her royalty.

Another woman took her place on the throne of the Bamum kings, and for a longer period of time. When Njoya's father died during one of the many wars that marked the history of the Bamum, Njoya was too young to rule. It was his mother, the fearsome Njapudunke, who took over as regent and governed the kingdom for thirteen years. Njapudunke is the most well-known of all the mothers of the Bamum kings. This is because she was the mother of the last real Bamum sovereign, but also because of her total involvement in the affairs of the kingdom. A skilled diplomat, she managed to diffuse conflicts, but did not shrink from war when necessary.

> For the war, Nə Nʒapnduŋke grumbled like a man. She spoke so loudly that a man listening to her seemed to be a woman before a man [...] Everyone, even foreigners, approved of her more than of the king.[19]

She was the one who advised the young Njoya to enlist the Fulani's help in order to defeat his opponents and maintain his hold on the throne. This was a queen known not for her passions in love but for her sense of duty. She threw all her strength into governing the kingdom, preparing the reign of her son and removing his enemies, definitively if need be. When Njoya was enthroned, she continued to support him, while taking care of her own affairs. Proprietor of twenty-three plantations, Queen Njapudunke was a wealthy woman whose suite counted nine thousand people. Her crops were so bountiful that she managed to feed the entire population of the kingdom during a period of famine, which means that she completely assumed the nurturing function of royal power. Converted to Christianity, Queen Njapudunke took the name of Elizabeth. She liked European-style buildings and objects. Ruthless in dispensing judgment as a regent, Njapudunke was reputed for her cruelty, as she did not hesitate to put to death those she found guilty. She was buried with her cleaver, one of the knives used throughout sub-Saharan Africa for executions or sacrifices. The pomp at her funeral was unimaginable, so numerous were the powerful who came to pay tribute to her, so great were the expenses dedicated to bringing her with honors to her final resting place.

As we can see, women are not totally excluded

from Bamum royalty. The law itself says so in no uncertain terms:

> Neither the king's nephew nor his brother can succeed him. If the king has no son, a daughter is chosen.[20]

She will thereafter be replaced by her son, provided that the father is of royal descent. If the princess has not yet given birth, a husband is chosen for her in accordance with regulations. A third woman, called Nsinsa, was queen of the Bamum, but her story is not told in "the book of the mothers of kings." Having evoked the women of the throne—be they guardians of the sanctuaries, sentinels assigned to the protection of the palace, princesses enjoying great sexual freedom, *momamfom* and especially de facto rulers—one wonders what the king could have meant in comparing himself to a woman in relation to the Germans. In the kingdom of Bamum as in other sub-Saharan societies, femininity was a richer, more complex notion than in Europe. Even among high-ranking women who did not have to work, femininity did not rhyme with physical weakness, fear of blood, softness and lack of authority. The mothers of Bamum kings, even the less well-known ones, often succeeded in acquiring and consolidating a fortune. The feminization that afflicted *mfom* Njoya had nothing to do with the feminine as it was understood among his people. It was mainly a political condition comparable to the social condition of ordinary women in a patriarchal society, a situation of impotence in decisions imposed on you by others. From this standpoint, Njoya was not the only one in this case. The systemic inequality that persists in the relations between Africa and Europe extends over present-day sub-Saharan peoples the debasement of their kings of the past. Royal objects that come from an invaded, overrun, plundered, alienated sub-Saharan Africa can be exhibited in Europe. But the treasures of European art do not travel to Africa. This is but one example of the difficulty in moving on from the colonial experience in an acceptable way. As long as the asymmetry between the great regions of the world that are Africa and Europe persists, things will not change. As for the Mandu Yenu, the throne of the Bamum kings named in honor of two women, let's hope that exhibiting it will lead to some knowledge of sub-Saharan women beyond clichés.

Translated from French by
Gila Walker

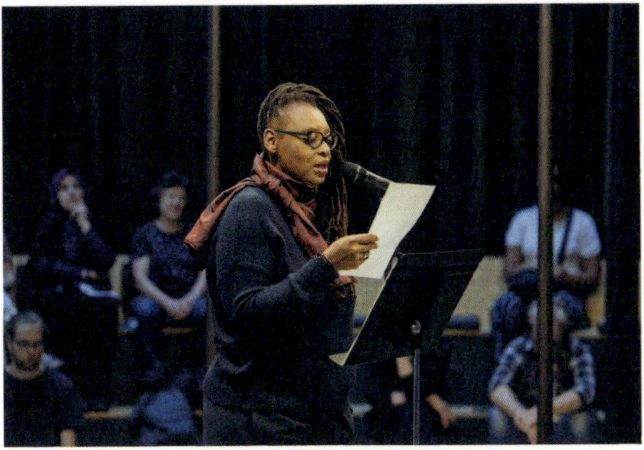

Léonora Miano at the Humboldt Forum

Notes

1 At the beginning of the twentieth century, two thirds of the Kingdom of Bamum was made up of servile people: the descendants of captives from the wars of the previous century or recent prisoners reduced to slavery. The servile condition can also be a sanction imposed for certain acts, such as opposition to the king. | **2** This was the name of the throne of the Bamum kings from the time of Mbuombuo, the eleventh monarch. | **3** This was the case in other regions of Cameroon. | **4** The chief title of Bamum kings, the term means "one to whom wealth comes effortlessly." | **5** He affably welcomed the Swiss mission from Basel. It was after its departure and also during the Great War—when the Christian nations fought among themselves—that his relations with this religion became conflictual, and this for a variety of reasons. See Nadeige Laure Ngo Nlend, "Le christianisme dans les enjeux de pouvoir en pays bamoun, Oeust du Cameroun, hier et aujourd'hui," *Études théologiques et religieuses*, vol. 88, no. 1 (2013), pp. 73–87. | **6** Claude Tardits, "Réflexions sur le sacrifice dans la religion traditionnelle des Bamoun (Cameroun)," *Systèmes de pensée en Afrique noire*, no. 4 (1979), pp. 117–129. | **7** Ibid. | **8** Aboubakar Njiasse Njoya, "The Mandu Yenu in the Museum för Völkerkunde Berlin," Baessler-Archiv, N. F. Bd. 42 (1994), p. 22. | **9** Christaud Geary, "Bamum Two-Figure Thrones: Additional Evidence," *African Arts*, vol. 16, no. 4 (1983), UCLA James S. Coleman African Studies Center, pp. 46–53, 86–87. | **10** Ibid., p. 48. | **11** Njasse Njoya, "The Mandu Yenu," p. 10. | **12** Claude Tardits, "L'étiquette à la cour royale bamoun (Cameroun)," *Publications de l'école française de Rome*, no. 82 (1985), pp. 179–198. | **13** Ibid. | **14** There was one exception at least to this rule with King Nguwuo, the fourteenth, but his reign was not well accepted and continues to be perceived as illegitimate. | **15** Tardits, "L'étiquette à la cour royale bamoun (Cameroun)." | **16** Sultan Njoya, ed., *Histoire et coutumes des Bamum*, trans. Henri Martin (Dakar: Mémoires de l'Institut français d'Afrique noire – Centre du Cameroun, 1952), 26:125. | **17** Ibid. | **18** Ibid., 26:126. | **19** Ibid., 27:133. | **20** Ibid., 71:189.

Credits

p. 5: bpk/Staatliche Museen zu Berlin, Ethnologisches Museum/Dietrich Graf | **p. 15:** © Grassi Museum für Völkerkunde zu Leipzig, Staatliche Kunstsammlungen Dresden, photo: archive | **p. 43:** Stiftung Humboldt Forum im Berliner Schloss, photo: Andreas König

The French original *Dames du trône*
by Léonora Miano is available online.

OBJECTS
TALK BACK

Priya Basil
Locked In and Out

Preface by Hartmut Dorgerloh
Paperback, 48 pages

Having recently accepted German citizenship, writer and activist Priya Basil explores the Humboldt Forum from a deeply personal perspective. She delves into the question of what such a building, such a project, means for an understanding of the past and our sense of belonging in the present. This much disputed, contested, celebrated monument now exists—but what exactly does it monumentalize? "In German the word *Schloss* means a palace, and also a 'lock.' The central question: Can a lock also be a key?"

OBJECTS
TALK BACK

Meena Kandasamy
A Wise One, a Warrior

Preface by Priya Basil
Paperback, 88 pages

Meena Kandasamy writes about the Mithuna couple, a seventeenth-century ivory sculpture from Tamil Nadu, India, depicting lovers. Kandasamy unfurls a multi-layered, multi-directional narrative built from images, questions and contradictions evoked by the sculpture. “How can we look at this work and not talk about who produced it?” Kandasamy asks and then examines how caste and class are carved into the object as indelibly as its physical details. Such knowledge complicates easy associations of love that may be evoked by the couple.
Refusing any impulse to idealize or exoticize, Kandasamy connects the carving to personal and political stories that expose painful realities of who gets to love whom, and how. She sets the intimate alongside the institutional to interrogate terms such as *decolonize, restitution* and *preservation*. Through an astonishing stylistic mix, including Twitter, academic discourse, poetry and memoir, she talks back, forward and sideways with the object.

Published by Stiftung Humboldt Forum im Berliner Schloss

Concept: Priya Basil
Project management: Katharina Kepplinger
Coordination and text editing: Susanne Müller-Wolff
Image editing: Barbara Martinkat

Special thanks to Fränze Czaja and Jan Linders (SHF) as well as to Jonathan Fine, Verena Rodatus, Maria-Antonie Ellendorff and the staff of the Ethnologisches Museum (SMB) for their friendly support.

www.humboldtforum.org

Die Beauftragte der Bundesregierung
für Kultur und Medien

Funded by the Federal Government Commissioner for Culture and the Media in line with a resolution by the German Federal Parliament

External links contained in the text could be reviewed only up to the publication date. The issuer and publisher have had no influence on later changes and can therefore accept no liability. The Deutsche Nationalbibliothek lists this publication in the Deutsche Nationalbibliografie; detailed bibliographic data are available on the Internet at http://dnb.dnb.de.

ISBN 978-3-0358-0755-4
Layout: 2edit, Zurich
Printing: Druckerei Vogl, Zorneding

DIAPHANES – Schöneggstrasse 5 – CH-8004 Zurich
DIAPHANES Berlin – Dresdener Strasse 118 – 10999 Berlin – kontakt@diaphanes.net